What do the fairies do with all those teeth?

To Joachim and Nicholas

No part of this publication may be reproduced in whole or in part, or stored in a retrieval system, or transmitted in any form or by any means, electronic, mechanical, photocopying, recording, or otherwise, without written permission of the publisher. For information regarding permission, write to Scholastic Canada Ltd., 123 Newkirk Road, Richmond Hill, Ontario, L4C 3G5, Canada.

ISBN 0-590-47264-X

French text copyright © 1989 by Michel Luppens.
English text copyright © 1991 by Scholastic Canada Ltd.
Illustrations copyright © 1989 by Philippe Béha.
All rights reserved. Published by Scholastic Inc., 730 Broadway, New York, NY 10003, by arrangement with Scholastic Canada Ltd.

12 11 10 9 8 7 6 5 4 3 2   3 4 5 6 7 8/9

Printed in the U.S.A.   08

First Scholastic printing, May 1993

What do the fairies do with all those teeth?

MICHEL LUPPENS

PHILIPPE BÉHA

English text by
JANE BRIERLEY

SCHOLASTIC INC.
New York Toronto London Auckland Sydney

Losing your first tooth is an important event.

They say if you hide it under your pillow, a tooth fairy comes in the night and takes it, leaving behind a few coins or a little gift.

But have you ever wondered what the fairies *do* with all those teeth?

YES! WHAT DO THEY DO?

Do they collect them just for the fun of it?

Do they string them into necklaces?

Do they choose the sharpest teeth to make their saws?

Or the roundest ones to make maraca sounds?

Perhaps they just make sets of false teeth?

Unless they choose the longest ones
to make their Halloween disguises?

Or the brightest to grind up into stardust . . .

Who knows? Maybe they take the most decayed, and get some witch to make a magic potion...

And by the way, do the fairies just collect *children's* teeth?

WHAT IF THEY VISIT THE ANIMALS, TOO...?